For Becca and Adam
XOXO, Mommy

For Chloe, my number one fan, and
Laurie Friedman, for creating Mallory, an
excellent role model for young girls
—J.K.

Oh Boy, Mallory

by Laurie Friedman

illustrations by Jennifer Kalis

MINNEAPOLIS

CONTENTS

A WORD FROM MALLORY

My name is Mallory McDonald, like the restaurant, but no relation. I'm ten and a half years old. I have red hair, freckles, a cat named Cheeseburger, an older brother named Max, and a best friend named Mary Ann.

I have fifty-three hair thingies, eight bottles of nail polish, twelve pairs of shoes (including old ones that don't fit and my fuzzy duck slippers), and a drawer full of T-shirts (which I can't count, because if I do, the drawer will get messed up and Mom will make me refold everything and I, Mallory McDonald, do not like to fold anything).

I have a shelf full of scrapbooks (most of them made by my best friend Mary Ann), a box of beads, another box of broken crayons,

6

and another box of old costumes (including an eggplant, a witch, and a musketeer).

I have a computer that I have to share with my brother Max (YUCK!) and a bathroom I also have to share with my brother Max (DOUBLE YUCK!).

I have a babysitter named Crystal who likes to give advice and a teacher named Mr. Knight who likes to give homework.

I have a lot of favorite things, including lemonade, doughnuts, peanut butter and marshmallow sandwiches, painting my toenails, saying things three times (with Mary Ann), and watching my favorite TV show, *Fashion Fran* (also with Mary Ann).

I have had appendicitis. I haven't had chicken pox.

And as of 11:42 this morning, I have a new diary, which is a good thing because as of the sleepover I went to last night, I, Mallory McDonald, officially have a lot to write about.

The Sleepover

SATURDAY MORNING, IN THE CAR WITH MOM ON THE WAY HOME FROM THE MALL

Dear Diary,

I'm not actually writing this in the car on the way home from the mall (I'm actually already at home on my bed with Cheeseburger), but if I had written it in the car (which I wouldn't have done anyway because writing in the car always makes me sick), here's what I would have written:

Dear Diary,

I just got you at the mall. I know. That

doesn't seem like the first thing you'd write about in a brand new diary. But here's something that is worth writing about: when Mom picked me up from the sleepover at April's house and I asked her if we could stop at the mall on the way home so I could buy a diary, she just said OK and did it.

I couldn't believe it.

She didn't ask any annoying mom sort of questions like: *Why do you need a diary? Did something happen? Is there something you want to talk to me about?* She didn't even say, *Can't you wait until we get home and just order one online?*

Nope. She didn't do any of the above.

She just said OK, pulled into the mall parking lot, went with me into the department store, and waited while

I picked you out, which took a while because there were a lot of diaries to pick from. I wanted a purple one because I love purple, but the purple ones had red stripes on them and I hate red so I got a yellow one with pink hearts on it, which was fine because I like yellow and pink. Then Mom drove me home and didn't say a word except for, "Mallory, please clean up your desk, and don't forget to change Cheeseburger's litter box."

The moral of the story: sometimes parents can surprise you, but not as much as friends.

Portrait of a mom who is not acting like a <u>mom</u>.

K.R.A.U.W.C.W.I.M. (That's short for Keep Reading and U Will C What I Mean.)

    X O X O, *Mallory*

    P.S. In case you're wondering what's up with the x's and o's, x=kisses, o=hugs, and it's how I sign all my letters (except ones I write to Max).

STILL SATURDAY, STILL ON MY BED, BUT HAVE ALREADY CLEANED UP MY DESK, CHANGED CHEESEBURGER'S LITTER BOX, EATEN A PEANUT BUTTER AND MARSHMALLOW SANDWICH, PAINTED MY TOENAILS, AND LOCKED MY DOOR SO MAX CAN'T COME IN AND TRY TO READ WHAT I'M WRITING

Dear Diary,

I have MEGA-BIG NEWS. It's also MEGA-TOP-SECRET NEWS!

A boy likes me.

You read it right, but just in case you blinked or couldn't believe what you read, I'll write it again.

A boy likes me.

At least, I think a boy likes me. Actually, I'm not really sure a boy likes me. All I know is that someone told me that a boy likes me.

The boy's name is Jake, and he's in fifth grade, and the someone who told me he likes me is Arielle. Actually, she didn't tell just me. She told Danielle (who I think already knew because Arielle and Danielle are best friends and tell each other everything) and Mary Ann and April and me. She told us all last night

at a sleepover at her house, which I was
kind of surprised I was invited to but
now I know why. She had something she
wanted to say, and she is the kind of
person who likes saying something when
she knows everyone will be excited to
hear it.

Seriously, when she said it, all my
friends started jumping up and down

and screaming like she'd just
announced the winner of a
beauty pageant. Then they
all started hugging me like I
was the winner.

"Mallory, it's so cool that
a boy likes you!" screamed
April.

"Mallory, it's so cool that
a super cute boy likes you!"
screamed Arielle.

"Mallory, it's so cool that a super cute
boy in fifth grade likes you!" screamed
Danielle.

"Mallory, say something!" screamed
Mary Ann.

But I wasn't really sure what to say, so
when everyone finished jumping up and
down and screaming about how cool it is
that a super cute boy in fifth grade likes

me, all I said was, "Are we still going to make s'mores?"

Danielle rolled her eyes, and Arielle groaned, and April slapped her head like there was something wrong with my head but since she couldn't slap mine, she slapped hers instead, and Mary Ann just mumbled that she couldn't believe I could think about my stomach at a time like this. And to be honest, I wasn't really thinking about my stomach. I was thinking about a lot of other things, but all the other things were kind of a jumble in my head, so s'mores just seemed like the easiest thing to think about.

xoxo,
Mallory

← Graham cracker

←marshmallow

← chocolate

← Graham cracker

Less complicated than boys.

P.S. Now that I've had some time to do some thinking, I know some of the things (besides s'mores) I was thinking about at the sleepover.

MALLORY MCDONALD'S LIST OF THINGS SHE WAS THINKING ABOUT AT THE SLEEPOVER (BESIDES S'MORES)

Thing #1: Even though my friends are excited about a boy liking me, am I excited about a boy liking me?

Thing #2: Do I even like boys? NOTE: I do like Joey (as a friend and next-door neighbor). I don't like Max (as a brother).

Thing #3: If a boy likes you, do you have to wear dresses and skirts and part your hair neatly?

Thing #4: If a boy likes you, do you have to cross your legs and sit up straight and chew with your mouth closed when you eat lunch?

Thing #5: If a boy likes you and you like him back, do you have to say nice things to him like, "Wow! You really threw that ball far!"

Thing #6: Do boys like to watch *Fashion Fran?* (I hope so.)

Thing #7: Do boys like to paint their toenails? (I hope not.)

Thing #8: If a boy likes you, does he give you presents? (I really hope so.)

Thing #9: If a boy likes you, do you have to give him presents? (I really hope not.)

Thing #10: How do you know for sure if a boy likes you and how do you know for sure if you like him back and how does he tell you he likes you and how do you tell him you like him back?

I know Thing #10 was actually four things and not one thing, but there are a lot of things (questions) I have and a lot of things (answers) I'm still looking for.

OK. G.2.G. (Got 2 Go.)

Mom is calling me, which probably means I have to do some homework, even though it's Saturday afternoon.

One last question: don't you think there should be a law against kids doing homework on Saturday afternoons?

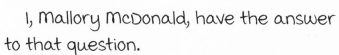

I, Mallory McDonald, have the answer to that question.

Y-E-S!

XOXO, Mallory

Mallory + Jake

WEDNESDAY AFTERNOON AFTER SCHOOL, ON MY BED WITH CHEESEBURGER AND A BAG OF OREOS

Dear Diary,

Do you know what a grapevine is? I'm not talking about the kind with little purple fruits that hang off of it.

I'm talking about the kind that passes along information. There's a

Not this kind of grapevine.

grapevine at my school that should be called the Jake → Ian → Olivia → Arielle → Danielle → Mary Ann → Mallory → Mary Ann → Arielle → Danielle → Olivia → Ian → Jake grapevine.

I bet you're curious what information this grapevine passed along, so I'll tell you. It passed along the Jake-likes-Mallory-and-Mallory-likes-Jake-back kind of information.

Confused how that worked? Well trust me, it was kind of confusing for me too (especially since most of the time that it was working, I wasn't actually there), but read on and hopefully you will get un-confused.

It all started Monday morning during fifth-grade P.E. (one of the times that I wasn't there).

During fifth-grade P.E., Jake told Ian (who is not only in his class but also on his baseball team) that he has a crush on me.

Jake   Ian

Then, Monday at lunch at the fifth grade table (another time I wasn't there), Ian told Olivia (his girlfriend) that Jake told him that he likes me.

Ian   Olivia

That night in the bedroom Olivia shares with her sister Arielle (yet another time I wasn't there), Olivia told Arielle that Ian told her that Jake told him that he likes me. If you're thinking that Arielle told Danielle because you already know that they're best friends and they tell each other everything, you're right.

Arielle   Danielle

So the next morning at school in our classroom before the bell rang (one of the times when I actually was there), Danielle told Mary Ann that she heard that Jake likes me. Of course, right when Mary Ann heard that, she told me what she heard. She waited for me to say something (like, "WOW! WOW! WOW! I LIKE HIM TOO!"), but I couldn't say anything because the bell rang and right when it did, my teacher, Mr. Knight, said to get out our math books and turn in last night's homework. So Mary Ann mouthed to me "T.B.C." which in case you don't know is short for To Be Continued.

Mary Ann Mallory

And it continued. Yesterday at lunch at the fourth-grade lunch table (another time when I was actually there), Mary Ann asked me if now that I know Jake likes me, do I like him back? I said I wasn't really sure. Mary Ann said she thought I should be sure and that since I wasn't, as my best friend, she would be sure for me. So Mary Ann told Danielle who told Arielle that I said I like Jake. Mary Ann also told me that I could thank her later, which I haven't done yet and still am not sure I want to.

Well, I bet you won't be too surprised to hear that that night, Arielle told Olivia what she heard. And I bet you also won't be surprised to hear that the next day at school, Olivia told Ian that she heard from a very good source that I like Jake. And if you're thinking that Ian told Jake that he heard through the grapevine that I like him . . . CONGRATULATIONS! YOU'RE RIGHT!

That's exactly what happened, and now (or so I heard) Jake knows (or thinks) that I like him back. So do you see what I mean about the information kind of grapevine?

I can't actually confirm that it all happened like I said it did because as I also said (and I said it a lot of times), most of the times that stuff was said, I wasn't actually there to hear what was said.

But I can confirm that what I told you is what I heard happened. OK.

I only promise this is what I heard.

That's it for now.

G.2.G. G.2.E.O. (Got 2 Go. Got 2 Eat
Oreos.)

X o X o, Mallory

Important Question
If Jake likes me and I like Jake, do
you think it's weird that the only two
people who haven't talked about it
are Jake and me?

On the Phone

THURSDAY NIGHT, AT THE DESK IN THE KITCHEN

Dear Diary,

Have you ever heard the expression "Ladies First"?

Well, what it means (or what I think it should mean) is that ladies go first, especially when it comes to using the computer they have to share with their brother.

In other words, I need to use the computer and since ladies go first, Max is going to have to wait. Here he comes.

G.2.G. G.2.M.S.T.L.G.F. (Got 2 Go. Got 2 Make Sure This Lady Goes First!)

X O X O, Mallory

THURSDAY NIGHT, STILL AT THE COMPUTER

Dear Diary,

This lady is going second. Max said he has to use the computer to do his homework. Mom said that doing homework is more important than emailing friends, and since that is what I said I was going to do, Max gets to use the computer. Then Mom said I have to do my homework too.

G.2.G. G.2.D.H.E.T.I. H.O.M.I.T.I.N.2.B.D (Got 2 go. Got 2 Do Homework Even Though I Have Other, More Important Things I Need 2 Be Doing.)

XOXO, Mallory

Homework or Email ?!?!

THURSDAY NIGHT, ON MY BED, SUPPOSED TO BE DOING MY HOMEWORK BUT LIKE I SAID, I HAVE OTHER, MORE IMPORTANT THINGS I NEED TO BE DOING

Dear Diary,

I'm sure you will understand when I tell you there is no way I can do my homework right now. Not when I have other, more important things I need to be doing, like talking on the phone. I don't know if you're the kind of diary who thinks a girl should do her homework before she talks on the phone, but let me tell you why, if that's the case, it's a silly way for you to think.

Today, as I was leaving school, Mary Ann told me she heard Jake is going to call me tonight and tell me he likes me, which will make him liking me "official."

well, he hasn't called yet. But if he does, I have to be ready, and the only way to be ready is to talk to Mary Ann and figure out what I'm going to say when he calls. So here's a question for you: how can I talk to Mary Ann before Jake calls if I'm doing homework? Now do you see what I mean about talking on the phone being more important than doing my homework?

I knew you would.

X o X o, Mallory

STILL IN MY ROOM, ACTUALLY DOING MY HOMEWORK

Dear Diary,

I went to the kitchen to use the phone and Mom said there was no way I could possibly be finished doing my homework and that I can't use the phone until she

sees signs (and by that she means math problems completed) that I've done my homework.

So that's what I'm doing.

XOXO, Mallory

<u>BACK IN MY ROOM, JUST GOT OFF</u> <u>THE PHONE</u>

Dear Diary,

I just got off the phone. First I talked to Mary Ann, then April, then Pamela, then Jake. I hope you aren't thinking, "Oh wow! She talked to everybody who is anybody! I can't wait to hear what she talked about." To be honest, my conversations weren't actually all that exciting, but since you're my diary, I'll tell them to you anyway.

First I talked to Mary Ann, and the conversation went something like this:

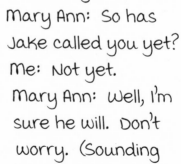

Mary Ann: So has Jake called you yet?
Me: Not yet.
Mary Ann: Well, I'm sure he will. Don't worry. (Sounding

worried.) I'm not worried. Are you worried?

Me: (Trying not to sound worried, but because of what Mary Ann said and the way she said it, starting to feel worried.) Who me? Worried? Not at all.

Mary Ann: The important thing to remember is that he's going to call, and when he does, he's going to tell you he likes you, so you need to be ready to tell him that you like him back.

Me: (Officially worried, as I hadn't thought about actually saying something like that to Jake.) Oh.

Mary Ann: OH!?! (Like she was waiting for me to say something else, like PIECE OF CAKE! I'LL TELL JAKE I LIKE HIM BACK! When I didn't say that, she kept talking.) Mallory, this is great! If Jake tells you he likes you, all you have to do is tell him you like him back, and then you'll be boyfriend and girlfriend, just like C-Lo and I are boyfriend and girlfriend, which means that you and I, as lifelong best friends, will have something else we do alike. It's just like painting our toenails the same color, or both saying things three times, or both liking *Fashion Fran*. Now, we'll both have boyfriends too. Do you get what I'm saying?

Me: (I got what Mary Ann was saying, but I wasn't sure how I was actually going to say to Jake that I liked him, which meant that Mary Ann and I might not have something else we do alike. Fortunately, I didn't

have to think about it for too long,
because I saw April's name on the
caller ID so I told Mary Ann I had to
go and I hung up.)

So then I talked to April, and here's
how that conversation went:

Me: Hey April. What's up?

April: I just wanted to tell you that
   I'm having a birthday party next
   Saturday night and I want to see if
   you can come.

Me: (Sounding happy because I love
   parties.) I'd love to come.

April: (Sounding happy too.) Great!
   I'm really excited. It's going to be
   lots of fun. I'll bring you an invitation
   tomorrow at school.

Me: I can't wait! See you tomorrow!
April: See you tomorrow!

Right when I hung up from talking to April the phone rang again. I thought (and kind of hoped) that it would be Jake (and was kind of relieved when it wasn't.) It was Pamela.

Pamela: Hey, Mallory, have you
   studied for the spelling test yet?
Me: Um, no, not yet.
Pamela: Want to quiz each other?
Me: (Telling Pamela that was what
   I wanted to do, but as soon as I
   started doing it, my brain stopped
   thinking about spelling words and
   started thinking about what Mary
   Ann and I talked about and if Jake

was going to call, and if he did, what he would say and what I would say.) DETERMINED.

Pamela: D-E-T-E-R-M-I-N-E-D. HANDKERCHIEF.

Me: H-A-N-K-E-R-C-H-I-F.

Pamela: Mallory, you need to study.

Me: (Looking down at the caller ID and seeing that Jake was on the phone.) Hey Pamela, I'm going to go study on my own for a while. Maybe we can do this later.

Pamela: OK. Bye.

Me: (Hanging up without even saying bye.)

So then I took a deep breath and answered Jake's call.

Jake: Hey, Mallory. It's Jake.

Me: Hey, Jake.

Jake: (Not saying anything like he's not sure what to say next.) So, what's up?

Me: (Not sure what to say next either but totally sure I shouldn't say what I was actually doing, which was waiting for him to say he likes me.) Not much.

Jake: Are you going to watch the game tonight?

Me: (Confused, because this was not what I thought he was going to say.) What game?

Max: (Who was not even part of this conversation, but unfortunately happened to walk into the kitchen right when Jake asked me if I was going to watch the game and heard

me say "what game?", groaned,
and said, "Could you be any more
stupid?" loudly enough for Jake to
hear him in the background.)

Jake: Hey, is that Max? Put him on.

me: (Handing Max the phone, even
though I knew that once I did,
Jake wouldn't tell me he likes me,
which I was sort of disappointed
about. But I also wouldn't have
to tell him I like him back, which I
was sort of relieved about. So I
just stood there and listened while
Max talked to Jake about some
baseball game. Then Max waved
his hand at me like I should get
lost, so I went to my room which is
where I am now.)

χοχο, Mallory

P.S. While I was going to my room (and I went kind of slowly), I heard Max and Jake talking and laughing like they had a lot to talk and laugh about.

Easier to understand than boys

STILL THURSDAY NIGHT, BACK ON MY BED

Dear Diary,

Just one more thing and one more question.

THE THING: Jake didn't actually say he likes me like Mary

Ann said he was going to. He didn't really say anything other than asking me if I was going to watch a baseball game.

THE QUESTION:
What do you think it means that Jake talked to Max more than he talked to me? I'm not sure what it means, but what I am sure about is that I'm NOT going to ask Mary Ann what she thinks it means, because what I don't want to hear her say is that my boyfriend likes my brother more than he likes me.

You don't think that's what it means, do you?

Of course not. You're my diary. You're not supposed to think things like that.

G.2.G. G.2.S.T.E.A.S (Got 2 Go. Got 2 Stop Thinking Except About Spelling.)

xoxo, Mallory

a Sign

FRIDAY AFTERNOON AFTER SCHOOL, AT THE KITCHEN TABLE EATING COOKIES

Dear Diary,

Even though I said wasn't going to ask Mary Ann what she thinks it means that the only thing Jake and I talked about last night was baseball and that he seemed more interested in talking to my brother than to me, it was the first thing I asked her when I saw her this morning.

Her answer surprised me.

She said it means absolutely, positively, 100% less than nothing and that there's only one little thing we need to do now, and that one thing is to wait for a sign.

I had a feeling she didn't mean the kind that sticks in the ground.

NOT THIS KIND OF SIGN.

So I asked her what exactly she meant and she said she was sure Jake likes me and that all we have to do today is wait for a sign that he does.

I asked her what that sign might be and she said that it could be any number of things that Jake might do when I'm looking. I had no idea what kinds of things Mary Ann was talking about, so I asked her and she told me.

♥POSSIBLE SIGNS♥ JAKE♥ LIKES ME (ACCORDING TO MARY ANN) ♥

Sign #1: Eating a banana in one bite.

Sign #2: Or an apple.

Sign #3: Squirting milk out his nose.

Sign #4: Balancing his lunch tray on his head.

Sign #5: Giving a big friend a piggyback ride.

Sign #6: Getting a piggyback ride from a little friend.

Sign #7: Running through the halls even though he's not supposed to.

Sign #8: Talking in the library even though he's not supposed to.

Sign #9: Talking in Chinese.

Sign #10: Or French.

I asked Mary Ann how we would know that any of these things mean Jake likes me.

She just laughed and said that if he did any of these things or any number of other things while I'm anywhere near him, it would be totally obvious that he likes me, and all we had to do was wait for him to do something.

So we waited.

We waited all morning. We waited during recess. We waited during lunch. We waited during library time. And we waited while the fifth graders were leaving the P.E. field and the fourth graders were going to the P.E. field.

Mary Ann said she thought that would have been an ideal time for Jake to give me a sign, especially since school was almost over.

When I said that maybe he isn't going to give me a sign, Mary Ann said not to think like that. She said she thinks Jake might be the kind of boy who likes to wait and give a girl a sign at the end of the day.

tick   tock

tick

tick

tick

tock

tock

The clock is ticking.

I told Mary Ann that at least April had given me an invitation to her birthday party so it wasn't like I was going home empty-handed.

When I said that, Mary Ann said that Pamela and Zoe and Arielle and Danielle and all the other girls in our class got invitations too. Then she wrapped her arm around me and told me not to worry, that she was sure I would be going home with an invitation and a sign.

To be honest, at the beginning of the day I wasn't actually worried. But as the day went on, I kind of started to worry, and the more the day went on, the more I just wanted a sign.

So finally, the bell rang and school was over. As I packed my backpack and got ready to go home, Mary Ann winked at me and said, "I bet Jake was waiting until the bell rings to give you a sign. We better go, so you don't miss it."

We grabbed our backpacks and walked towards the gates of Fern Falls Elementary. We walked really slowly because Mary Ann said we wouldn't want to leave before Jake had a chance to leave and give me my sign.

But guess what, we were the last ones to leave school and still no sign. In fact, no sign of Jake at all. I could tell Mary

World's slowest walkers.

Ann felt bad for me because she came over to me and said, "Who cares about a stupid sign anyway?"

I nodded like I agreed, but the truth is, I cared.

X O X O, Mallory

Once Upon a Time

SATURDAY AFTERNOON, AT THE WISH POND

Dear Diary,

I hope you don't mind stories where the author doesn't tell you how the story ends, because I'm about to tell you one.

Once upon a time there was a sweet, cute girl who had a cat, a dog, a brother, two parents, her own room, a lifelong best friend, a favorite TV show, and as of late, a boy who was maybe her boyfriend but she wasn't 100% sure because she had heard he liked her, but she hadn't heard it from him. She had always led a nice, simple life until she heard this boy liked her and that's when things got complicated.

Girl leading the simple life.

Here's what happened.

One day (this morning, actually), this cute, sweet girl got a call from the boy she heard liked her.

When she heard his voice, she felt two things.

One was happiness.

She had been waiting for a sign that he liked her and right when she heard his voice, in her heart she knew this was a sign and that it was an even better sign than if he had squirted milk out of his nose or talked in Chinese.

The other thing she felt was surprised.

The reason she felt surprised is because the boy asked her a question that she wasn't expecting him to ask her. And when she's surprised, she can't do her best thinking, which is exactly what happened next.

What a Surprise!

The boy asked her if she would like to come to his birthday party. He told her that the party was next Saturday night and that it's a pool party at his house.

Like I said, the girl was surprised when he asked her if she wanted to go to his party next Saturday night, and also like I said, when the girl is surprised, she can't do her best thinking. So when he invited her to his birthday party, she said, "Yeah, sure, I'd love to come."

Then she hung up the phone, and as soon as she did, she started thinking a little better.

Right then, she remembered that she couldn't go to his party next Saturday night because she had already told her friend April that she would go to her party next Saturday night.

Then she did what any girl who was

once again doing her best thinking would do. She picked the phone back up and called her lifelong best friend, Mary Ann, to ask her how she should tell the boy that she can't go to his party.

My brain doing its best thinking.

And that's when her best friend went completely CRAZY!
"You can't NOT go to Jake's party!" the girl's best friend said. "Since he

invited you to his party that means you're going out... that makes him your boyfriend... this is so cool... you have to go."

The sweet, cute girl thought about what her best friend said. But it didn't make a lot of sense to her that just because she got invited to Jake's party, she was going out with him. Also, she had already told her friend that she would go to her party so she couldn't NOT go. She tried explaining all of this to her friend.

I can't hear you!

But her friend refused to listen.

All she said was that she was going to the mall to buy new underwear and as soon as she got back she was coming over to fix the girl who in her opinion obviously needed some fixing.

The sweet, cute girl didn't exactly know what it was about her that needed fixing, so she hung up the phone even more confused than when she picked up.

THE END (which as I told you at the beginning is really not an ending).

X o X o, Mallory

Dr. Mary Ann

<u>STILL SATURDAY AFTERNOON, IN
MY ROOM IN MY BED WHICH IS
WHERE MARY ANN SAID I NEEDED
TO BE</u>

Dear Diary,

Mary Ann or I should say Dr. Mary Ann just left.

She crawled in my window about twenty minutes ago. She said she came over to make sure I wasn't sick, and the place she said she thought I might be sick is in the head.

Right when she came over, she made me get into bed.

Then she checked my eyes, my ears, my nose, and my throat. She even felt my forehead to see if I had any fever.

The Sick Ward.

"You look fine, but you're definitely not acting fine," said Mary Ann. "Even thinking about not going to Jake's party is a sure sign of not-fine-ness."

"But I can't go to Jake's party when I've already told April I'd go to her party," I said.

When I said that, Mary Ann said I absolutely could go to Jake's party, and that all I had to do was un-tell April I was going to her party.

"It's not that simple," I told Mary Ann. "I want to go to Jake's party. But I want to go to April's party too." I sighed like I was faced with a big dilemma, because I am. "I wish I could be at both parties at the same time," I told Mary Ann.

Mary Ann made a thinking face, which is what she makes when she's thinking.

Then she snapped her fingers like she had a good idea. "Why don't you go to Jake's party and I'll go to April's party dressed as you?"

Will the real Mallory please stand up?

I shook my head like that would never work. "You'll already be at April's party dressed as you," I reminded Mary Ann.

Mary Ann said I was right about that, and since I couldn't be two places at one time, the place I should want to be is at

Jake's party. Then she made her sick-of-listening-to-me face, which is the face she makes when she's sick of listening to me.

Then she started talking like she meant every word she was saying.

"Mallory, it's so cool that Jake invited you to his party, and I'm sick of listening to you tell me you can't go. If you don't go, I'm going to think you're a little sick and also a little crazy. All you have to do is tell April you can't come to her party."

"If I tell her I can't come to her party because I'm going to another party, I'm going to hurt her feelings."

Mary Ann rolled her eyes. "Then make up a reason why you can't go to her party."

Even though I wasn't really sick, I starting to feel a little sick when Mary Ann said that. But before I could tell Mary Ann that I didn't like the sound of what she was saying, she put her hands on the sides of her head like she just had a brainstorm.

"Tell April you're having a family thing and that your parents said you have to stay home that night," said Mary Ann.

I frowned. "What kind of a family thing?" I asked.

Mary Ann rolled her eyes again like she shouldn't have to answer that question. "Say anything. Say it's your grandmother's birthday and you have to be home to help her celebrate."

I frowned again.
I felt like the kids in
The Cat in the Hat.

Mary Ann's plan
did not sound like
a good one. "What
am I going to tell my
parents?" I asked.

"Have you already told them about
April's party?" asked Mary Ann.

I shook my head no, that I had not.

"OK. So it's simple. Just tell them
you're invited to Jake's party."

"I haven't even told them about Jake,"
I said.

Mary Ann rolled her eyes a third time.
Then she rubbed them like she was
scared they might get stuck like that.
"So tell them about Jake, and then tell
them you're invited to his party."

I shook my head. "I don't want to lie to April," I said.

Mary Ann crossed her arms and shook her head like I was being a difficult patient and she was done with this conversation. "I'm the doctor and I gave you a prescription. Now all you have to do is follow it." Then Mary Ann said the doctor visit was over and she went right back out the window she came in.

When she left, I felt my forehead. Doctors are supposed to make you feel better, but I feel worse than ever.

$\chi o \chi o$, Mallory

SUPER COOL that I'm invited to a fifth-grade boy's birthday party. They said I'm probably one of the few fourth-grade girls in the history of Fern Falls Elementary to be invited to a fifth-grade boy's party. Danielle said that means if someone wrote a history book about Fern Falls Elementary, I would be in it.

Historical photo of fourth grader, Miss Mallory McDonald, attending a fifth grade boy's party, circa 2012.

A Poem,
By Miss Mallory McDonald

I was going to a party.
Then I got invite #2.
That's one invite too many
NOW I DON'T KNOW WHAT TO DO!!!

My friend has an opinion.
I'm not sure I agree.
But I feel like if I don't
She'll think that I'm CRAZ-EEE!

How will I decide?
Should I wait for a sign?
Whose opinion counts the most?
My best friend's or mine?

HeADS or tAILs ??

Eenie, Meenie, Miney, Go

Dear Diary,

I have to make a decision about whose party I'm going to on Saturday night, but I'm having a very hard time making that decision.

Mary Ann thinks it should be a simpl decision. Today at school she told Arie and Danielle that Jake invited me to birthday party (and surprise, surpri they already knew) and that I'm th about not going.

At lunch, they all told me that

I told Danielle that I'm not sure I want to make history.

But she said what she is sure about is that Jake wouldn't have invited me to his party if he didn't like me. Then she shook me by the shoulders like she was trying to shake some sense into me and she said, "MALLORY, YOU HAVE TO GO AND I MEAN IT!" Then she and Arielle and Mary Ann all gave me looks like they meant it.

We mean it!

Then she told me that I didn't have to worry about any of them saying anything to April because they already made a pinky swear not to say a word to April.

Honestly, that didn't make me feel much better because a) from past experience, I know that Arielle and Danielle are not the world's best secret keepers, and b) now it is sort of like four people are lying to April and not just one.

Do you see why I'm having trouble deciding what to do?

Last summer I watched this really old movie with Grandma called *Gone with the Wind*. When the main character, Scarlett O'Hara, has trouble deciding what to do, she says "I'll just think about that tomorrow."

A Poem,

By Miss Mallory McDonald

I was going to a party.
Then I got invite #2.
That's one invite too many
NOW I DON'T KNOW WHAT TO DO!!!

My friend has an opinion.
I'm not sure I agree.
But I feel like if I don't
She'll think that I'm CRAZ-EEE!

How will I decide?
Should I wait for a sign?
Whose opinion counts the most?
My best friend's or mine?

Eenie, Meenie, Miney, Go

MONDAY NIGHT ON THE COUCH, TRYING TO WATCH *FASHION FRAN* BUT HAVING A HARD TIME FOCUSING ON FASHION OR FRAN

Dear Diary,

I have to make a decision about whose party I'm going to on Saturday night, but I'm having a very hard time making that decision.

Mary Ann thinks it should be a simple decision. Today at school she told Arielle and Danielle that Jake invited me to his birthday party (and surprise, surprise, they already knew) and that I'm thinking about not going.

At lunch, they all told me that it's SO

SUPER COOL that I'm invited to a fifth-grade boy's birthday party. They said I'm probably one of the few fourth-grade girls in the history of Fern Falls Elementary to be invited to a fifth-grade boy's party. Danielle said that means if someone wrote a history book about Fern Falls Elementary, I would be in it.

Historical photo of fourth grader, Miss Mallory McDonald, attending a fifth grade boy's party, circa 2012.

I told Danielle that I'm not sure I want to make history.

But she said what she is sure about is that Jake wouldn't have invited me to his party if he didn't like me. Then she shook me by the shoulders like she was trying to shake some sense into me and she said, "MALLORY, YOU HAVE TO GO AND I MEAN IT!" Then she and Arielle and Mary Ann all gave me looks like they meant it.

We mean it!

Then she told me that I didn't have to worry about any of them saying anything to April because they already made a pinky swear not to say a word to April.

Honestly, that didn't make me feel much better because a) from past experience, I know that Arielle and Danielle are not the world's best secret keepers, and b) now it is sort of like four people are lying to April and not just one.

Do you see why I'm having trouble deciding what to do?

Last summer I watched this really old movie with Grandma called *Gone with the Wind*. When the main character, Scarlett O'Hara, has trouble deciding what to do, she says "I'll just think about that tomorrow."

I'm going to do what Scarlett did, and think about that tomorrow.

XOXO, Mallory

TUESDAY NIGHT, IN BED, CURLED UP NEXT TO CHEESEBURGER

Dear Diary,
I bet you're waiting to hear what I decided to do about the parties this weekend.

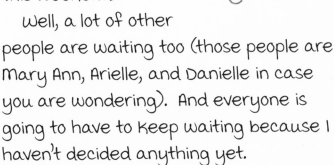

Well, a lot of other people are waiting too (those people are Mary Ann, Arielle, and Danielle in case you are wondering). And everyone is going to have to keep waiting because I haven't decided anything yet.

I want to decide. But I can't. I tried making a PROS and CONS list.

Which party should I go to?
? PROS vs. CONS ? ?

April's Party

Pro: It would be fun.
Con: I would have to miss
      Jake's party.

Jake's Party

Pro: It's cool that I'm invited.
Con: I'd have to miss April's party.

But my pros and cons list wasn't very
helpful.

I even called my babysitter, Crystal,
who has a real crystal ball. When she
looks into her ball, she says she can see

the future. She looked into her ball for me and said she could see me at a party. When I asked her whose party, she said her ball can't tell one party from another. Then she said that if I wanted to tell her what is going on, she would be happy to give me some advice.

World's most useless Crystal ball.

But I don't need advice. I need to make a decision.

XOXO, Mallory

WEDNESDAY MORNING BEFORE SCHOOL, IN MY BATHROOM DOING MY HAIR

Dear Diary,

I made a decision.

Actually, it's a plan to make a decision. Here's my plan. If the cafeteria serves pizza for lunch, I'm going to April's party. If they serve chicken fingers, I'm going to Jake's.

G.2.G. I.L.U.K.W.O.T.M. (Got 2 Go. I'll Let U Know What's On The Menu.)

XOXO, Mallory

Pizza vs. Chicken

WEDNESDAY AFTERNOON AFTER SCHOOL, AT THE DESK IN THE KITCHEN

Dear Diary,
It was hot dog day.

X o X o,
Mallory

NOT helpful with decisions

Well, I'm still at the desk in the kitchen. April just called and I just hung up from talking to her. Our conversation wasn't good at all. It wasn't bad, but it wasn't a conversation that I was having fun having. Do you know what I mean? Well, if you don't, read what we talked about and I think you'll get it.

April: (Sounding happy) Hey Mallory, just two more days till my party.

Me: (Trying to sound happy) I can't wait!

April: I'll tell you one of the surprises at the party if you'll swear not to tell anybody.

Me: (Not sure what to say because feeling terrible that April wants to tell me about a surprise that's going to happen at her party that I might not even be at.)

Max: (Who is not even part of this conversation, but walked into the kitchen while I was having it.) Mallory, get off the phone. I need it.

Me: (Trying to sound upset that I can't stay on to hear April's secret and trying to hide my own secret

which is that for once I'm glad my
brother thinks he can use the phone
whenever he wants it.) Sorry April,
I've got to give the phone to Max.

April: OK. The secret can wait. See
you tomorrow.

Max: (Grabbing the phone out of my
hand and looking at me like I just
ate the rest of last night's dessert
and didn't leave any for him.)
What's going on, Mallory? I've never
seen you get off the phone so fast.
You're definitely up to something.

Me: (Leaving the kitchen, which is the
best way to ignore my brother when
I don't want to answer his question.)

OK. Now I'm back in my room. Max is definitely wrong. I'm not up to something. What I'd like to be up to is making a decision, and I'm definitely not up to that.

But what I have decided is that I have to decide soon. Tomorrow is Thursday, and the day after tomorrow is Friday, and the day after the day after tomorrow is Saturday, which as of now is the day I'm going to two parties.

I just decided. I'm going to look for a sign. Tomorrow I'm going to look for a sign, and when I get it I'm going to make my decision. It's decided.

XOXO, Mallory

THURSDAY NIGHT, ON THE FLOOR OF MY CLOSET WITH THE DOOR CLOSED SO NO ONE CAN SEE WHAT I'M WRITING

. Dear Diary,

I made my decision.

Well, it kind of got made for me.

Here's what happened. Just now, when Mom came to tuck me in, she smiled and said, "A little birdie told me that a certain fifth-grade boy likes a certain fourth-grade girl."

For once, I was totally happy that Mom is the music teacher at my school and sort of knows what goes on. I felt like she was giving me the sign I'd been waiting for.

In my head, I could see Mary Ann and Arielle and Danielle telling me to go to Jake's party. And even though part of me really wanted to go to April's, I did what any girl in my position would do. I said to myself, "Eenie, Meenie, Miney ... Go!"

And just like that, I made my decision.

I decided to go to Jake's.

So I told Mom that Jake likes me and that he invited me to his birthday party on Saturday night and I asked her if it would be OK for me to go.

Mom smiled again. "Of course it's OK."

Then we talked a little bit about Jake and the party and what time it starts and ends and where it is and Mom never said anything like, "Are you invited to any other parties that night?" So I never said anything back like, "There's a tiny

problem, which is that I was invited to another party, and I already said yes, so I'm going to have to say that you said I can't go because it's Grandma's birthday, and even though I wish I could go, you're making me stay home and celebrate with my family."

I didn't say any of that. I just said, "Nighty-nite," which is what I say when Mom tucks me in.

XOXO, Mallory

Is she as sweet as she looks?

FRIDAY AFTERNOON AFTER SCHOOL, AT THE WISH POND

Dear Diary,

I came out to the wish pond to make a wish. I'm going to find the best rock I can find. I'm going to close my eyes. And I'm going to throw the rock in the wish pond and make a wish that I made the right decision.

Hold on. I'm going to do it now . . . .
. . . .

OK. I just did it. I hope it works.
I guess we'll see soon enough.
Saturday night, to be precise.
Wish me luck.
    X o X o, Mallory

Party Prep

SATURDAY NIGHT, ON MY BED, ABOUT TO LEAVE FOR JAKE'S PARTY

Dear Diary,

I'm leaving in a few minutes to go to Jake's party. But before I do, I have three things to tell you.

Thing #1: Mary Ann says when she grows up she wants to be a celebrity stylist.

You're probably wondering why it's important for me to tell you this before I go to Jake's party, or what makes Mary Ann think this is something she would be good at, so I'll tell you both.

Mary Ann just spent the last two hours styling me. She curled my hair and painted my nails and did my makeup and picked out my outfit.

And when she was done, she said, "You look fabulous dah-ling!" She said that's what celebrity stylists say to their clients when they're done getting them ready.

When I looked at myself in the mirror, I told Mary Ann I'm not so sure that's what stylists say or that I look fabulous,

but Mary Ann said she's the stylist and she knows what they say and that she knows I look good.

Thing #2: Mary Ann says when she grows up if she doesn't become a celebrity stylist, she's going to become a relationship guru.

Honestly, I had never even heard of a relationship guru, but Mary Ann says that a guru is someone who is an expert, and a relationship guru is someone who is an expert on how to have good relationships. She said she's seen them on TV, and that since she's been in a relationship with C-Lo since the beginning of fourth grade, she thinks she could be one.

She said this because she gave me some advice and she thought her advice was great. To be honest, I have no idea if it is great or not.

The advice she gave me is that I should hold hands with Jake at the party.

I told her I have absolutely no idea how to hold hands with a boy at a party.

She said I don't need to do anything.

Then she told me about Operation Sit Next To Jake So He'll Hold My Hand. She said all I have to do at the party is sit on the couch next to Jake, leave my hand on the couch, and wait for Jake to hold it.

Like this?

Thing #3: I feel like I swallowed a bag of Cheese Curls. And I'm not just talking about what's inside the bag. I'm talking about the bag itself.

CHEESE CURLS!

There are lots of reasons why I feel this way. A) I'm not sure I like the way I look. B) I'm even less sure I want to sit next to Jake and put my hand on the couch so he will hold it. C) When Mary Ann left a little while ago, she said, "Have fun at Jake's. That's what I'll be doing at April's." To be honest, even though Mary Ann and Arielle and Danielle all said how cool it is that I'm going to Jake's party, I can't help wishing I was going to April's instead. D) I feel terrible about not telling Mom and Dad about April's party, and E) I feel even worse (if that is even possible) about lying to April about having to stay home to celebrate my grandmother's birthday.

Mom is calling me.

It's party time.

XOXO, Mallory

The Party

Dear Diary,

I'm writing so fast, my fingers are flying.

Faster than a speeding plane!

I'm writing fast because I just got home from Jake's party and Mom and Dad said I have exactly five ~~months~~ (oops, I mean minutes) to put on my

97

pajamas and brush my teeth before I have to report to their room.

A lot has happened since I wrote in you last (even though I didn't write in you all that long ago). Like I said, I don't have a lot of time, so I'm going to make a long story short:

I'm in **BIG** TROUBLE!

I don't actually have enough time right now to tell you about all the **BIG** trouble I'm in, so I'll tell you about the party instead.

It was not fun.

In case you read that wrong, read again: the party was NOT fun.

I had a terrible time. If I was telling Mary Ann about it and not you, I would say, "I had a terrible, terrible, terrible time." Here's why:

When I got to the party, Jake was

playing basketball outside with all the boys, so I went inside where all the girls were, but all the girls were older so I didn't really know them except for Arielle's older sister, Olivia. But she sort of pretended not to know me, so I had to pretend not to know her back. And none of the girls really talked to me (actually, they didn't talk to me at all), so I didn't really talk to them.

Also, all the girls were wearing their hair down and cover-ups over their bathing suits, and I was wearing my hair in a side ponytail and a skirt and ruffly top over my bathing suit, so all the other girls kept giving me why-are-you-wearing-a-side-ponytail-and-a-skirt-and-ruffly-top-over-your-bathing-suit looks.

While the older girls were busy not talking to me and looking at me, I went

What is she WEARING?

and sat on the couch by myself. (Actually, I wasn't totally by myself. I had a plate of chips and dip.)

Anyway, I spilled some dip on my skirt and I tried to wipe it off, but it left a big, ugly spot.

O O P S !!!

Then, after I had been sitting alone
with chips and dip and staring at the
spot on my ruffly skirt and thinking for
what felt like forever that Mary Ann
should not be a celebrity stylist when
she grows up, someone yelled, "Pool
time!" and everyone raced outside and
started jumping in the pool and splashing
each other and laughing like they
liked it.

I started splashing too, but some
girl that I don't know told me to stop
splashing her.

I wanted to splash Jake but he and his
friends were busy doing cannonballs into
the deep end and making gorilla noises
while they did it.

So, I kind of hung out in the pool by
myself and tried to look like I was having
fun even though I wasn't.

After we were done swimming,
everyone went back inside and hung out
some more. Everyone was laughing and
talking and having a good time. Everyone
but one person, and that one person was
me. I didn't have anyone to talk to or
laugh with so I got more chips and dip and
went and sat by myself on the couch.

While I was eating my chips and dip,
I thought about all of my friends at

April's party laughing and talking and having a good time.

Lonely girl food

Then I tried not to, but I couldn't help thinking about all of my friends at April's party laughing and talking and having a good time without me.

It made me so sad to think about it that I almost choked on a chip.

I didn't think anything could happen that could make me have a worse time than I was already having, but just then, something did.

When Jake's mom brought out a birthday cake and everyone gathered around the table to sing happy birthday to Jake, the doorbell rang.

Who could it possibly be?

Jake's dad went to get it, and you will never believe who was at the door.

What I am about to tell you is so hard to believe, I won't even make you guess. It was Mom and Dad!

Mad Parents!

That's right! It was my mom and dad, and to be honest, they did not look happy.

I watched while Jake's dad talked to them. Then they motioned for me to come with them. So I followed them out of Jake's house and that is where the BIG trouble began.

But more on that later. I hear Mom calling me. I think my five minutes are up.

XOXO, Mallory

P.S. If you're wondering how Operation Sit Next To Jake So He'll Hold My Hand went, you can stop wondering. In case you didn't notice, I never actually sat next to Jake.

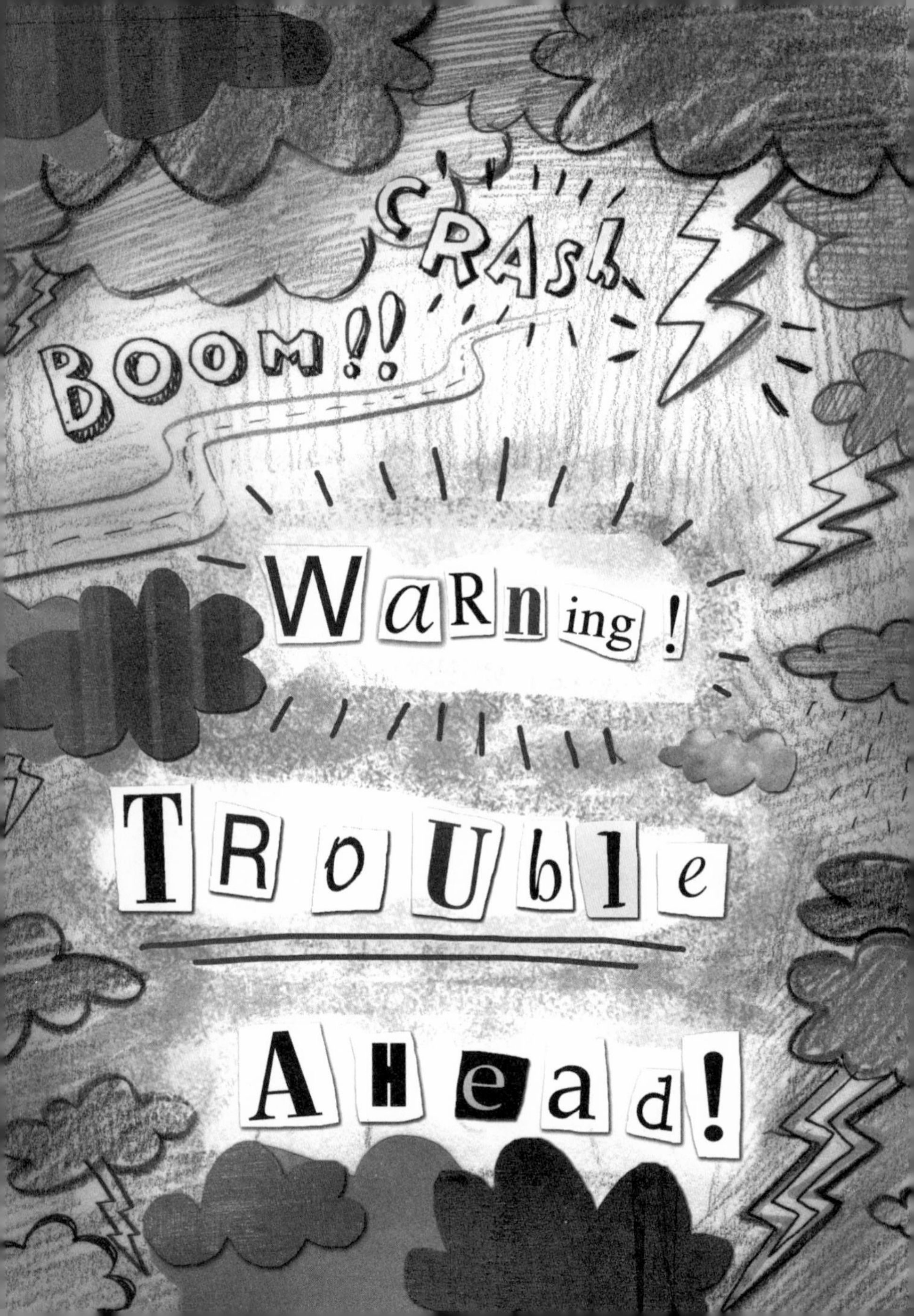
CRASh
BOOM!!
WaRning!
TRoUble
AHead!

BIG Trouble

BACK IN MY ROOM, MUCH, MUCH, MUCH LATER BECAUSE I HAD A LONG, LONG, LONG TALK WITH MOM AND DAD IN THEIR ROOM

Dear Diary,

First things first . . . I have never been so happy to be back in my own room. Being in Mom and Dad's room (where I usually like being unless I'm in trouble, which I was tonight) was not fun at all.

But before I tell you what happened in their room, I'll tell you what happened in the van on the way home from Jake's party and I'll also tell you this . . . it wasn't good.

Remember when I told you I followed Mom and Dad out of the party? Well, I followed them straight into the van, and

as soon as I got in, they started talking.
Here's what they said:

    Mom: Mallory, we are very upset with
        you.

    Dad: Mallory, a lot of people are upset
        with you.

    Me: (Not saying anything like "Who is
        upset with me?" because I knew I
        wouldn't have to ask Mom and Dad
        to tell me who was upset with me. I
        knew they were planning to tell me.
        Plus, I sort of had an idea who they
        were going to say but I crossed my

toes that I would be wrong.)

Mom: We got a call a little while ago
from April's mom asking if there
was any way you could come to
April's party for cake and ice cream
when we finish your grandmother's
birthday dinner.

Me: (Still not saying anything, but
uncrossing my toes because my
toe-crossing wasn't doing any good.
I was right about who I thought they
were going to say.)

Mom: (Looking at me and not in a
very nice way.) So, of course,
I told April's mom that we were
not having a birthday dinner for
your grandmother. I told her your
grandmother's birthday isn't for
another two months and that you
were at Jake's birthday party.

Me: (Still not saying anything, but
     pretending to be at the wish pond
     on my street and wishing that there
     was a magical way to wish back
     what my mom said to April's mom.)

Sometimes a girl just needs
a little abracadabra.

Mom: (Interrupting my wish, which
      in my opinion is what made it not
      come true.) Then, April's mom
      told me that there must be some
      confusion, because April told her
      that you said you couldn't go to
      April's party because you had to
      stay home to have dinner with

your grandmother on her birthday.
(Mom and Dad both turning around
to look at me like it was my turn to
talk. So I did.)

Me: Dad, don't you think you should
be looking at the road and not me
while you're driving?

Mom: Mallory, we're almost home,
and when we get there, you have
exactly five minutes to put on your
pajamas and brush your teeth.
Your father and I want to see you
in our room. You're in **BIG** trouble,
young lady.

The End.

Well, that was the end of what
happened in the van. I'm going to take a
little break because my hand is too tired
to keep writing.

But when I come back, I'll tell you what happened in Mom and Dad's room.

T.B.C. (To Be Continued...)

XOXO, Mallory

Sore hand

ON MY BED, CURLED UP NEXT TO CHEESEBURGER

Dear Diary,

My hand is rested so I'll tell you what happened in Mom and Dad's room. They were *very, very, very, very, very, very, very, very, very, very* (I'm going to quit writing "very's" because I'm sure you get what I'm talking about, but trust me, I could keep writing "very's" for a very long time) upset with me for lying to April.

I tried to explain to them that I felt like I had to go to Jake's party and that I didn't really want to lie to April. I tried to explain to them that I told April I had to stay home to celebrate my grandmother's birthday because I thought that would not hurt her feelings, but that if I had told her I picked Jake's party over her party, I would have hurt her feelings.

I thought for sure (actually, I didn't think for sure, but I hoped maybe) my parents would be proud of me for finding a way not to hurt April's feelings, but they weren't proud at all.

"Mallory, you lied to April," said Mom. "And I'm sure lying to her made her feel worse when she found out than if you had told her the truth in the first place."

When Mom said that, I felt worse too.

WORSE is me!!!

"Mom, Dad," I said to my parents. "The truth is, I didn't really want to go to Jake's party, but I felt like I had to go because Mary Ann and Arielle and Danielle kept saying how cool it was that I was invited to it, so I went. And I didn't even have a good time. The whole time I was there, I kept thinking about all my friends having fun at April's party and I kept wishing I could be there instead of at Jake's."

When I said that, Dad sat down on the bed next to me and he had a very serious look on his face.

"Mallory, lying to other people is wrong. You owe April an apology."

Dad's Serious face.

I nodded like I got what Dad was saying, but he kept talking anyway. "And it's equally important to be honest with yourself. You knew what you wanted to do, but instead of listening to yourself, you listened to what other people told you that you should do."

Dad paused again, so I nodded again.

Then Dad talked for a *very, very, very, very, very,* (I know, you get the whole "very" thing) long time about

listening to my heart and how, as I grow up, I should do what I think is right for me and not what other people think is right for me.

Then I told Dad that growing up is not always easy.

I told him that when I was younger and I did something wrong, he and Mom would punish me. But now that I'm older, I feel like knowing I did something wrong to someone else is worse than any punishment they could have given me.

Dad put his arm around me, but he didn't take the serious look off of his face. "Mallory, it never feels good when we hurt someone's feelings."

"Tomorrow, I'm going to call April and apologize," I told Mom and Dad.

They told me that they are proud of me for doing the right thing.

I told them that I'm going to do it, but that I'm not looking forward to it.

Mom and Dad nodded and said they understood.

So tomorrow I'm going to apologize to April. I don't think it's going to be easy. I wonder if it would be easier in Chinese or French?

I have a feeling apologizing is hard no matter what language you do it in.

XOXO, Mallory

"a" Is for...

SATURDAY MORNING, AT THE WISH POND

Dear Diary,

"A" is for April and apology and an invitation.

This morning, after I woke up, fed Cheeseburger, made my bed, brushed my hair ninety-two times on each side, re-folded all of my T-shirts (and in case I haven't told you this yet, I hate folding), and ate a pomegranate, which takes longer to eat than any other food on the planet, I decided

One fruit that can't be rushed!

that sooner or later I would have to call April and it might as well be sooner. So I called her to see if I could come over.

When I called, April did not sound too happy to hear from me. "You didn't want to come to my party last night, so why do you want to come to my house today?" she asked.

I told April that I felt really bad about last night and that I wanted to apologize.

April still did not say OK. She just said, "Hmm." So I asked again, and she said, "I'm not sure."

I thought about what Dad said about how it never feels good when we hurt someone's feelings. I could tell that April was really upset with me, and I was not feeling good at all.

So I told her again that I felt really, really, really bad about what happened and that I really, really, really wanted to apologize, and that I had something I wanted to give her.

When I said that, April said I could come over after lunch. So, that's what I'm going to do. But first I have to talk to Mom about an idea that I have. Then, I have to talk to Mary Ann, Arielle, Danielle, Pamela, and Zoe. Then, I have something I have to make.

I.K.U.P. (That's short for I'll Keep U Posted.)

XoXo, Mallory

SATURDAY AFTERNOON, BACK AT THE WISH POND

Dear Diary,

I just got back from April's house. I bet you can't wait to hear what happened so I'll tell you. But first I'll tell you this: on a scale of 1 to 10, my visit started out as a 3 and then dropped down to a 1 (keep reading and you'll see why).

April was REALLY, REALLY, REALLY upset that I didn't go to her party!

Even after I explained to her what happened and told her that I wished I had been at her party because I know I would have had a lot more fun at her party than at the party I went to, April told me she was still mad at me for not telling her the truth about where I was going.

I told her I didn't blame her for being

mad. I also told her that I should have been honest with her and that I was sorry I wasn't.

See what I mean about my visit starting out as a 3? Things weren't going so well, and then they got worse.

At this point in our conversation, two unexpected things happened. The first one was that April started crying. I've never seen April cry, but she told me she was really mad and upset with me. Then, to make things worse, April's mom came into April's room where we were talking. She had a big plate of brownies. (I could tell they were fresh out of the oven because they had that delicious fresh-out-of-the-oven smell.)

I think she was just about to ask us if we wanted one, but when she saw April crying, she handed April a tissue and asked her if she was OK. April said that she and I had a lot to talk about, so April's mom nodded and left with the brownies.

Now you see why things went from a 3 to a 1?

I waited for April to wipe away her tears, and then I told her that I know I wasn't a good friend to her on her birthday and that I was sorry, but that I wanted to make it up to her. Then I reached into my purse and gave April what I made for her this morning.

April looked at me like she wasn't sure what it was, so I told her it was an invitation.

She said she could see that, but she wasn't sure what it was an invitation to. So I told April that she should open it up to see what was inside.

Then I crossed my toes that she would like what was inside and waited while she read it. It seemed like it took April a

really long time to read what was inside
the envelope, but I know it couldn't have
been that long because I kept my toes
crossed the whole time she was reading,
and I am NOT good at keeping my toes
crossed for long. (Mary Ann is excellent
at it.)

When April finished reading, she looked at me like she didn't understand, so I explained.

"I felt really bad that I missed your birthday party, so I want to have another one for you. Next Saturday, you are cordially invited (I know, I sounded like an invitation when I said this) to my house for a best-ever post-birthday celebration. I invited Mary Ann and Pamela and Arielle and Danielle and Zoe too. They're all coming, and we're going to spend the whole day doing super fun birthday things."

When I finished explaining all this, April got a huge smile on her face and said that that sounded like a great idea.

I told her I was really glad she liked my idea and that I had another great idea, which was eating some brownies.

Lucky for me, April thought that was a good idea too.

So my visit that started as a 3, and went down to a 1, ended up a 10.

XOXO, Mallory

129

Breaking Up

SATURDAY AFTERNOON, AT THE DESK IN THE KITCHEN

Dear Diary,

When I got home from April's house, I decided there were a few more people I needed to talk to. The first one was Mary Ann.

Even though I had told her that I wanted to have a post-birthday celebration for April, I never told her what happened at the party and about my talk with Mom and Dad.

After I told her everything, I told her that I'm always glad she's my best friend, but that sometimes I have to listen to myself and not her.

Mary Ann didn't have a lot to say about that.

Then I told her that even though I wasn't 100% sure Jake and I were ever really going out, I decided I'm going to break up with him.

That's when Mary Ann started talking.

She told me that was a CRAZY idea because Jake is super cute.

But I told her that I don't really care how super cute he is, that I don't really like having a boyfriend all that much.

Then Mary Ann told me that breaking up is hard to do. She said there's some old song her parents listen to that's all about it.

She said I'd better find a good way to tell Jake because people don't like it when you break up with them. She said sometimes they cry and beg you not to do it, and sometimes (she said she has seen this on TV), they even go crazy or have a breakdown or make you say 100 times why you're breaking up with them.

I don't want Jake to cry or beg or go crazy or have a breakdown, and I especially don't want him to make me say 100 times why I'm breaking up with him, so I'm going to look online to find good things to say to a boy when you're breaking up with him.

CRAZY JAKE!

B.R.B.A.I.F.S.T.a.S. (That's short for Be Right Back After I Find Some Things a Say.)
X O X O, Mallory

STILL AT THE DESK IN THE KITCHEN

Dear Diary,

Here are some of the things I found:

THINGS TO SAY TO A BOY WHEN YOU'RE BREAKING UP WITH HIM
1. It's not you, it's me.
2. I need a change in my life.
3. I wish we had met five years ago. (Although, I would have been five, so I think I will change this to: I wish we could meet five years from now.)
4. I don't want to hold you back.
5. Sometimes life throws us a curveball. (Note to self: this one's really good since Jake is a pitcher.)

But I didn't think those things sounded perfect, so I also made up some of my own things:

MORE THINGS TO SAY TO A BOY WHEN YOU'RE BREAKING UP WITH HIM
1. My cat has been sick and needs my attention.
2. I might be getting sick. (Note to self: cough when saying this.)
3. My parents are making me do this.
4. I'm changing my hairstyle, so I'll be busy for a while.
5. I think you'd really like my cousin Jennie.

I can't decide which thing I want to say when I tell Jake it's over, so I'm keeping both lists handy. I guess I'll know what to say when I tell him ... which I'm going to do right now.

But first, I'm going to close my eyes, pretend like I'm at the wish pond, and make a wish that Jake won't cry or beg or go crazy or have a breakdown or make me say 100 times why I'm breaking up with him.

OK. I made my wish. Now, I'm going to do it. Wish me luck.

XOXO, Mallory

STILL AT THE DESK IN THE KITCHEN

Dear Diary,

I did it.

I just talked to Jake and told him that I'm breaking up with him. You might be surprised to hear this, but he didn't cry or beg or go crazy or have a breakdown, and he definitely didn't ask me to repeat 100 times why I'm breaking up with him.

In fact, he didn't ask me to repeat anything.

Here's what happened when I called him:

Me: Hey Jake, there's something I need to tell you.

Jake: Is it about the baseball game? It starts in five minutes.

Me: It doesn't have anything to do with baseball. It has to do with us. I think we should break up. (Me pausing, deciding which thing to say about why we should break up...)

Jake: (Before I even have a chance to say why we should break up.) Cool. Can you get Max? I want to ask him who he thinks is going to win.

Me: (Checking my ears to make sure they heard right and wondering if

Jake should check his.) So, like I
said, we should break up. OK?

Jake: Yeah. Whatever. So is Max
there? I really want to talk to him
about the game.

Me: (Completely shocked that Jake
could think about baseball at a time
like this.) I'll get him.

So that was it. I got Max. Jake talked
to Max. Max watched the game. I guess
Jake watched the game too.

The truth is . . . I don't really know what
he did because we broke up and we
didn't talk after that.

And here's some more truth . . . I'm
not even sure we were ever really even
boyfriend and girlfriend, or official, or
together, or whatever you want to call it.
It's not like we ever said that we were.

138

And hey, here's even more truth . . .
even when we were together or
whatever it was, the only thing we talked
about was baseball, and let's be honest,
Jake talked to Max about it a whole lot
more than he ever talked to me.

So here's the last bit of truth I'll share
with you on the subject of having a
boyfriend. Breaking up isn't all that hard
to do. And that's the
truth according to me.
    XOXO,
Mallory

This stuff makes you
tell it like it is.

Friends forever

Happy Birthday

Recipe for a Perfect Day

SATURDAY NIGHT, IN THE BATHTUB

Dear Diary,

Here's the recipe for a perfect day:

RECIPE for <u>A Perfect Day</u>!

INGREDIENTS:

<u>Friends</u>   <u>Fun</u>

<u>Food</u>   _____

DIRECTIONS:

Invite your friends over. Plan lots of fun things to do. Include something yummy to eat. Mix together and enjoy!

P.S. I thought it would be fun to write in you in the bathtub, but it was actually more wet than it was fun. T.B.C. (To Be Continued.)

SATURDAY NIGHT, IN BED WITH A FLASHLIGHT

Dear Diary,

I have to use a flashlight to write in you because Mom said after the busy day I had, I have to get some sleep.

Mom is right about one thing. It was a busy day, but it was a fun one. Mary Ann said, "It was really, really, really fun." Zoe, Arielle, Danielle, and Pamela said they had a great time. I did too. And best of all, I think April had a lot of fun.

Today, they all came over for April's best-ever post-birthday celebration, and

esn't sound like I'm bragging, but I
ink it was the best birthday lunch ever.
inly I think this because when April bit
her sandwich, she said it was the
t birthday lunch ever. The truth is,
ryone loved it.

ary Ann said it was "Super-duper
a tasty."

e said she was going to tell her mom
wanted the same thing for dinner.
elle, Danielle, and Pamela all loved it.
n Max, who came into the kitchen
we were making the sandwiches
te one, said it was the best
ich he'd ever tasted. (That means
to be good because Max almost
ikes anything I make.)
utting in the recipe so I never, ever
t.

we spent the whole day doing birthday
things.

First, we played birthday games in the
backyard.

We had a jump rope contest and
a Hula-Hoop contest and a hopscotch
contest and a skipping contest and a
crazy dance contest.

April "won" all of the contests because
it was her birthday and she got all of
the prizes. At first Mary Ann thought it
wasn't fair, and she was acting kind of
pouty and mad. But Pamela, Zoe, and
I, and even Arielle and Danielle, thought
it was fair, so Mary Ann finally stopped
being pouty and mad (especially when I
reminded her that she didn't have time
to pout because she was supposed to be
taking pictures).

Official Winner

Official Photographer

After all the contests, we played Pin the Tail on the Dog. We wanted to play Pin the Tail on the Donkey. We tried to draw a big picture of a donkey to hang on a tree, but Arielle and Danielle thought our picture looked more like a dog than a donkey, so we just decided to play Pin the Tail on the Dog. Guess who won? (If you said April, you were right.)

After that, we filled up a jar with jelly beans and we all tried to guess how

many jelly beans were in the knew how many were in it u them out and counted them won? If you said April, you right and half wrong. Pam had the closest guess (she there were 329), but since celebrating April's birthday, she gave the jar of jelly beans to April.

When we finished playing birthday games, we had a birthday lunch.

We made peanut butter, ban honey, and marshn I came up with the

do
thi
ma
int
bes
eve
m
extr
Zo
she u
Ari
Eve
while
and a
sandu
it had
never
I'm p
forget

144

146

we spent the whole day doing birthday things.

First, we played birthday games in the backyard.

We had a jump rope contest and a Hula-Hoop contest and a hopscotch contest and a skipping contest and a crazy dance contest.

April "won" all of the contests because it was her birthday and she got all of the prizes. At first Mary Ann thought it wasn't fair, and she was acting kind of pouty and mad. But Pamela, Zoe, and I, and even Arielle and Danielle, thought it was fair, so Mary Ann finally stopped being pouty and mad (especially when I reminded her that she didn't have time to pout because she was supposed to be taking pictures).

Official Winner

Official Photographer

After all the contests, we played Pin the Tail on the Dog. We wanted to play Pin the Tail on the Donkey. We tried to draw a big picture of a donkey to hang on a tree, but Arielle and Danielle thought our picture looked more like a dog than a donkey, so we just decided to play Pin the Tail on the Dog. Guess who won? (If you said April, you were right.)

After that, we filled up a jar with jelly beans and we all tried to guess how

many jelly beans were in the jar. Nobody knew how many were in it until we took them out and counted them. Guess who won? If you said April, you were half right and half wrong. Pamela actually had the closest guess (she said 287 and there were 329), but since we were celebrating April's birthday, she gave the jar of jelly beans to April.

Property of April.

When we finished playing birthday games, we had a birthday lunch.

We made peanut butter, banana, chocolate chip, honey, and marshmallow sandwiches. I came up with the recipe. I hope this doesn't sound like I'm bragging, but I think it was the best birthday lunch ever. Mainly I think this because when April bit into her sandwich, she said it was the best birthday lunch ever. The truth is, everyone loved it.

Mary Ann said it was "Super-duper extra tasty."

Zoe said she was going to tell her mom she wanted the same thing for dinner.

Arielle, Danielle, and Pamela all loved it.

Even Max, who came into the kitchen while we were making the sandwiches and ate one, said it was the best sandwich he'd ever tasted. (That means it had to be good because Max almost never likes anything I make.)

I'm putting in the recipe so I never, ever forget it.

R E C I P E for

The Best Birthday Sandwich Ever!?!

Ingredients:

Bread

Peanut butter

Banana slices

Chocolate chips

Honey

Mini marshmallows

Frilly toothpicks

directions:

Lay out two slices of bread. Spread peanut butter on one slice. Top with sliced bananas, chocolate chips, and mini marshmallows. Squirt honey on other slice of bread. Close up sandwich, cut into quarters, and stick a frilly toothpick in each quarter. Eat and enjoy!

After we ate the birthday sandwiches, we had birthday cake. It was chocolate with rainbow sprinkles and a big candle. Mom helped me make it. We all sang happy birthday to April, and then she made a wish and blew out the candle.

She said she's never gotten to celebrate her birthday twice in one year and that she liked it so much that when she made her birthday wish, she wished she could do it again next year.

After we ate cake, we all watched back-to-back episodes of *Fashion Fran* before my friends went home.

When April left, she hugged me and told me it was the most fun post-birthday celebration ever. I told her I was really glad she liked it, and I did too. The truth is . . . it was a lot more fun than the last birthday party I went to.

And guess what, tonight when Max said to me to not even think about going on the computer, that it was his turn, I just said OK.

I know he thought I was going to argue with him and tell him why it was my turn, but I told him that I was so tired from all the fun I had with my friends today, that he could use the computer for as long as he wanted.

He said he's going to remember that and that I'll be lucky to ever get another turn.

Well, that's it for now. I'm 2.T.2.W.A. (That's short for 2 Tired 2 Write Anymore.) And as for getting the computer back, in the words of Scarlett O'Hara . . . I'll think about that tomorrow.

X o X o, Mallory

Photos

ON THE FLOOR OF MY ROOM, GLUING PHOTOS INTO MY DIARY

Dear Diary,

Here are some cute pics that Mary Ann gave me from April's post-birthday celebration.

Here's a picture of all my friends doing the crazy dance contest.

Here are some pictures of Mary Ann dancing. She was the official photographer, but since she couldn't take pictures of herself, I took these.

Here's a picture of April pinning the tail on the dog.

And here's a picture of all my friends with April while she's blowing out the candle on her cake.

Mom took this one, and when she took it she said, "There's nothing nicer than spending the day with your friends."

I have to say that I, Mallory McDonald, absolutely, positively, 100% agree.

XOXO, Mallory

a Quiz

<u>AT MY DESK, DOING SOMETHING
THAT WILL BE HELPFUL TO GIRLS
EVERYWHERE EVEN IN FOREIGN
COUNTRIES LIKE ICELAND AND
ALASKA (WHICH I THINK IS A
COUNTRY, BUT I'M NOT 100% SURE)</u>

Dear Diary,

I'll be the first to admit that when it comes to boyfriends, having one was something I thought I wanted. OK, I wasn't really sure it was what I wanted, but my friends thought it was what I should want so it made me think maybe it was what I wanted too. But I learned a few things:

One: It wasn't at all what I wanted.

Two: No one can decide what you want except for you. (I know, I sound like

Dad, but in this case, I think he actually knows what he's talking about.)

Three: I wish I'd had something (like a fairy godmother or a crystal ball that actually worked) to help me make that decision, but I didn't.

Since there was nothing to help me, I've decided to help other people by creating this simple quiz, which, in my opinion, makes the *do-you-really-want-a-boyfriend* question really simple to answer.

DO YOU REALLY WANT A BOYFRIEND?
By Mallory McDonald

Dear Quiz Taker,

If having a boyfriend is something you're thinking about, I've created this simple quiz to help you decide if it's something you're ready for. I really hope this quiz helps you make your decision. And even if it doesn't, I hope you have fun taking it. By the way, quizzes are always more fun when you take them with a friend. So buddy up! Also, I should probably tell you that I'm not a doctor or a relationship guru so the following quiz isn't scientifically proven. It's just the best I could think of. Have fun!

Do these statements sound like you? Answer YES or NO for each one.

1. I spend a lot of time thinking about one particular boy.
2. My friend has a boyfriend and it makes me want one too.
3. Lots of my friends have boyfriends which makes me think I should have one.
4. I like talking about boys with my friends.
5. I think I'm too young to have a boyfriend.
6. I'd rather spend time with one boy than lots of girls.
7. When I go online, the first thing I do is check to see if one particular boy is online.
8. At school, I try to look my best so one boy will notice me.

9. If a boy I like likes something I'm not interested in (like baseball), I would be happy spending my free time learning about it.

10. I would rather talk to a boy on the phone than watch my favorite TV show.

YES: If you answered YES to six or more questions, I think you're ready for a boyfriend. Remember, I told you I'm not a relationship guru, but it seems like boys are something that don't completely gross you out (unlike meatloaf or creamed spinach, both of which I promise are completely gross).

NO: If you answered YES to fewer than five questions, I don't think you're ready for a boyfriend. And don't feel bad about it... I took the quiz myself and only had two YES's (and one of them was #5.) I think the important word here is YET. As in... You're not ready for a boyfriend YET.

MAYBE: If you answered YES to 5 questions and NO to 5 questions, I have absolutely no idea if you are ready for a boyfriend or not. You could try flipping a coin or better yet, make a peanut butter, banana, chocolate chip, honey, and marshmallow sandwich, which I promise is tons more fun than flipping a coin or having a boyfriend!

Whatever it is you decide to do, I hope you have fun doing it!
X O X O, Mallory

Carolrhoda Books
A division of Lerner Publishing Group, Inc.
241 First Avenue North
Minneapolis, MN 55401 U.S.A.

Website address: www.lernerbooks.com

Cover background © iStockphoto.com/Tio.

Main body text set in Swister 17.5/20.
Typeface provided by The Chank Company.

SUSTAINABLE
FORESTRY
INITIATIVE

Certified Chain of Custody
Promoting Sustainable
Forest Management
www.sfiprogram.org

Library of Congress Cataloging-in-Publication Data

Friedman, Laurie B., 1964-
    Oh boy, Mallory / by Laurie Friedman ; illustrated by Jennifer Kalis.
        p.   cm. — (Mallory ; #17)
    ISBN: 978-0-7613-6072-8 (trade hard cover : alk. paper)
    [1. Dating (Social customs)—Fiction. 2. Diaries—Fiction.] I. Kalis, Jennifer, ill.
II. Title.
PZ7.F897730h 2012
[Fic]—dc22   2011022320

Manufactured in the United States of America
1 – SB – 12/31/11